This book belongs to

....

Written by Katherine Sully
Illustrated by Frank Endersby

© 2014 Alligator Publishing Limited, London, England.

Published by International Greetings USA, Atlanta, GA 30342

Printed in India.

Hen's Feathers

Hetta and Hilda were sisters, but not from the same clutch of eggs. Hetta was older than Hilda.

Hilda had plump, shiny black feathers, sunshine yellow legs and beak, and a beautiful red comb.

Hetta was dull and brown. But, she was very kind and took good care of Hilda.

Every morning, long after the rooster had crowed, the hens all waddled out of the henhouse looking for their breakfast.

Hilda was very popular with the other hens. She was always in the middle of the crowd, clucking about this and that.

On this particular morning, there was a new
hen in the yard. She had fluffy, white feathers.
Soon, everyone crowded around to meet her.

The new hen's name was Chantelle.
Everyone cooed and clucked, "What a pretty
name!" What's more, Chantelle had won a
prize at the farm show. Everyone wanted to
be her friend.

Except Hilda. Hilda sulked.

"Chantelle's prettier than me," grumbled Hilda. "And she's more popular!"

"Don't be silly, Hilda," said Hetta. "You're just as pretty as Chantelle, but in a different way."

The next morning, Hetta couldn't find Hilda anywhere. Then, she spotted the other hens all crowded around Chantelle. She went over to see if Hilda was there.

"You'll never guess what," Chantelle was saying, "…the fox is back!"

There was no sign of Hilda. Now, Hetta was really worried—Hilda could be in big trouble if the fox was back!

Hetta rushed all around the farmyard
looking for Hilda.

"Have you seen
Hilda?" she asked
the pig. But, he was
too busy eating
to reply.

"Have you seen
Hilda?" she asked the
farm cat. But, she was
too rude to even reply.

"Have you seen Hilda?" she asked
the rooster.

"She was around earlier," he crowed,
"disturbing me while I was preening
my feathers!"

Hetta went back to the farmyard just in time to see Hilda. She had rooster feathers stuck to her head and tail and was strutting around the henhouse.

The other hens were giggling behind their wings. Even Hetta had to admit that Hilda looked silly!

That night in the henhouse,
Hilda was very angry.

"I don't know why everyone
thinks Chantelle's so
wonderful," she
snapped.

Hetta looked at her sister. "Chantelle
is a very nice hen, Hilda," said Hetta.

"Just because her feathers
are perfect!" grumbled Hilda.

The following morning, the hens were
all in a flutter. During the night, the fox
had been back, and eggs were missing! The
hens gathered outside the henhouse. Hetta
looked around. Hilda was missing too!

"Look, over here!" called Chantelle. She had spotted rooster feathers near a hole in the fence. They crowded around gasping and worrying. It was clear to everyone – the fox had taken Hilda.

The hens did their best to comfort Hetta.

"She was a lovely hen," they clucked. "The best sister you could have wished for."

Hetta was heartbroken!

Just then, Hilda turned up – wearing peacock feathers. She looked ridiculous! But this time, no one was laughing – they were too angry!

That night in the henhouse, Hilda was very upset.

"I just wanted everyone to notice me!" she hiccupped.

"You don't need all these peacock feathers, Hilda," Hetta clucked gently.
"We all love you just as you are…"

Suddenly, they heard scuffling and squawking…

Hetta and Hilda rushed out of
the henhouse to find the
fox with Chantelle...
...IN HIS MOUTH!

As quick as a flash, Hilda
plucked a long peacock feather
from her tail and tickled the fox's nose.

The fox froze. His nose twitched, his eyes squeezed shut and…
…ATCHOO!

Chantelle shot from his mouth and escaped.

The next morning, the hens
gathered to hear about the night's events.
Hetta smiled to herself as she spotted Hilda.
In the middle of the crowd was her sister with
her wing around Chantelle.

"…and that's the best use for a peacock
feather I know," chuckled Hilda as she told
the story to her crowd of admirers
one more time.

The End